Moyes

A PARRAGON BOOK
Published by Parragon Books, Unit 13-17 Avonbridge Trading Estate,
Atlantic Road, Avonmouth, Bristol BS11 9QD
Produced by The Templar Company plc, Pippbrook Mill,
London Road, Dorking, Surrey RH4 1JE

Designed by Janie Louise Hunt
Edited by Caroline Steeden
Printed and bound in Italy
ISBN 1-85813-941-4

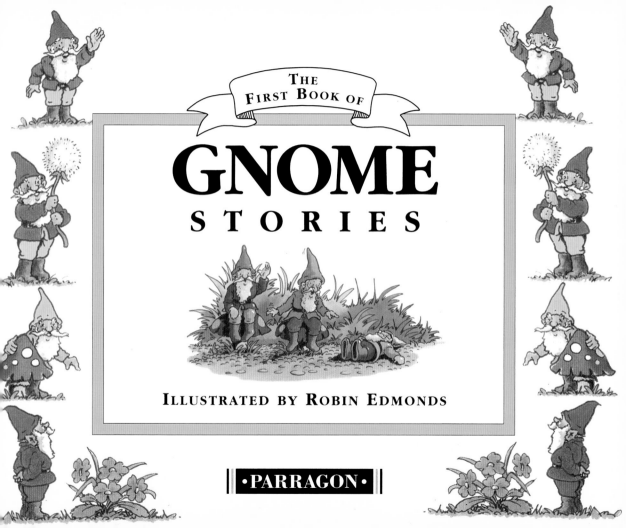

THE
FIRST BOOK OF

GNOME
S T O R I E S

ILLUSTRATED BY ROBIN EDMONDS

||·PARRAGON·||

This Book Belongs to

_____

_____

CONTENTS

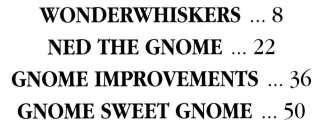

WONDERWHISKERS

WRITTEN BY GEOFF COWAN

Down among the plants and shrubs, in many a garden, you may come across a little painted stone figure with a bushy white beard and red, pointed hat. Often as not, he's sitting on a toadstool or fishing with a tiny rod. These little folk are, of course, garden gnomes. If you've seen one, then you'll know what a real gnome looks like.

Well, Wonderwhiskers was no different, except for his beard. It was the thickest, strongest and longest you could imagine. In fact, it was so long that Wonderwhiskers had

to part it down the middle and, with the help of other gnomes, roll it up into two bundles which he carried on his back.

Any sensible gnome would have cut such a beard and, in the early days, Wonderwhiskers had tried to. But by next day, it had always grown longer than before.

"Amazing!" he'd gasp, as he stared at his beard in the mirror. So he decided he'd just have to live with it.

Besides, Wonderwhiskers was very proud of his beard. It had made him famous! The other gnomes treated him with the greatest respect, and would do anything he asked them. There wasn't a gnome in the land who hadn't invited him home for a slap-up meal. Oh, yes! Wonderwhiskers was definitely a V.I.G., a Very Important Gnome. But it had not always been like that…

There was a time when Wonderwhiskers had been just

your average common-or-garden gnome, by the name of Norman. He had lived in a snug underground home beneath an old storm-struck tree, deep in the heart of the forest. Norman and his gnome neighbours would go in search of tiny treasures to decorate their home, such as shiny pebbles, a lucky four-leaved clover or even a fluffy feather, dropped by one of their bird friends.

That, however, was before Norman's beard had begun to grow and grow. Before long it became a bit of a nuisance. The end would blow into Norman's face so that he couldn't see where he was going. Once, Norman had walked straight into his friend Tiggletum who dropped a sackful of forest treasures on his toe. Even after Norman began to roll up his beard, it sometimes came loose and dragged along the ground, like the time when his cousin Lightstep tripped on it and went flying into a puddle.

Yet, every night before he went to bed, Norman always washed and brushed his beard before measuring it to see just how much longer it had grown. Such a big, bushy beard made him feel special.

"The bigger his beard, the bigger Norman's head!" others began to utter with just a teensy-weensy hint of jealousy as word spread of his incredible beard, and visitors came from far and wide to see it.

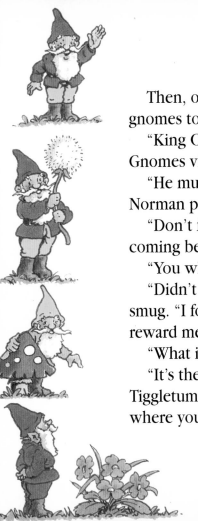

Then, one day, some unbelievable news caused the gnomes to chatter excitedly.

"King Cracklecorn's coming! Imagine! The King of the Gnomes visiting us!" cried Norman's neighbours.

"He must have heard about my beard, too," said Norman proudly.

"Don't flatter yourself," replied Tiggletum. "He's coming because I wrote to him!"

"You what?!" gasped Norman.

"Didn't I tell you?" continued Tiggletum, looking oh-so-smug. "I found the rarest treasure of all. The king's sure to reward me!"

"What is it, this treasure?" asked Norman.

"It's the place where the rainbow ends," announced Tiggletum. "Every gnome knows it's a magical place, where you'll find a pot of gold!"

14

"Why didn't you bring the gold back with you?" asked another gnome, called Bizzybonce.

Tiggletum shuffled his feet and looked awkward. "Well, I think I've found the rainbow's end," he explained. "One sunny afternoon last week I went out for a walk, but it began to rain. A rainbow appeared. I saw one end dip towards a clearing. I ran all the way there but, by the time I arrived, the rain had stopped so the rainbow vanished. But I should be able to find the spot again!"

"I hope so!" frowned Lightfoot. "Fancy inviting the king without being sure!"

It was too late for Tiggletum to start worrying now. Before they knew it the king was on the doorstep and they all set off to find the rainbow's end. By the time they had covered half the forest and walked in circles for a few hours, everyone was feeling grumpy, especially the king.

To make matters worse, it began to rain. No sun, mind you; just rain, rain and more rain. As they hurried back to their homes, they decided to take the short cut beside the brook. But it had swollen to a fast-flowing stream and that's when the king had an accident. He slipped, fell in and was nearly washed away.

"Someone fetch a rope!" yelled Tiggletum, as King Cracklecorn clung to a piece of driftwood that, for a lucky moment, had jammed between two rocks amid the rapids.

"We don't have a rope! We don't have anything that can save him!" cried Bizzybonce.

"Oh, yes we have!" replied Norman. He unrolled his beard which he'd kept neatly behind his back as usual. Next moment, he threw the end to the king who managed to grasp it.

"Hold on, your Majesty!" called Norman. Turning to the others, he said, "Hurry! Help me pull him towards us!"

Inch by inch, through the surging water, the King of the Gnomes was pulled closer. Norman closed his eyes, bit his lip and never uttered a sound, although it must have been very painful. After all, imagine how hard his beard was being tugged! Ouch!

But, at last, helping hands lifted the weary king clear and he sat puffing on the riverbank. Soaked but safe, he turned to Norman.

"I hereby name you Wonderwhiskers," he said thankfully, "and grant you the title of S.M.I.G!"

"Second Most Important Gnome," whispered Tiggletum to the others in amazement. "That means only the king is more important than Norman, I mean Wonderwhiskers, now!"

They all thought he had been incredibly brave and clever. As they went to congratulate him, they slipped on his dripping beard, toppled into each other and landed in a happy heap. Everyone laughed, including the king.

And from that day on, the invitations poured through Wonderwhiskers' letterbox. He spent his time enjoying one visit after another, to tell his famous story or show off his fabulous beard. His admiring hosts did everything they could to make such a noble gnome feel comfortable.

As Wonderwhiskers often joked to himself, it was just like home from home … or gnome from gnome!

NED THE GNOME

WRITTEN BY AMBER HUNT

Ned the Gnome spent the morning sticking his feet into icky sticky mud puddles and breathing deeply the horrible smell that accompanies icky sticky mud. He tried to tell himself he loved the mud and adored the smell, but he didn't, not really … not even a little bit. Eventually, feeling quite down in the dumps, Ned went and sat on the top of a little hill, wondering what he was going to do.

"Excuse me," said a voice behind him, "but why don't you smell?"

"What?" said Ned, startled. "Why should I smell?"

"I asked a question first," replied the voice, "and you can't answer a question with a question. It's rude. But then you're a gnome, so I suppose rudeness is all that can be expected from you ... so why don't you smell then?" Ned turned to see a rabbit peeking its head out of a burrow behind him.

"Well, that's the problem," said Ned. "Not that it's any of your business, but I don't like dirt and mud and I hate being rude to people."

"I see," scoffed the rabbit. "A clean, polite gnome. I suppose you expect me to believe that, do you? All gnomes are rude, dirty and smell horrible." The rabbit sniffed loudly. "I don't like gnomes, never have and never shall."

"Oh," said the gnome. "Well, what makes you think rabbits are so perfect, always digging holes for us little folk to fall down?" and so saying, he turned his back on the rabbit.

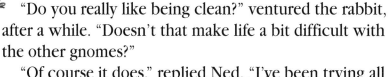

"Do you really like being clean?" ventured the rabbit, after a while. "Doesn't that make life a bit difficult with the other gnomes?"

"Of course it does," replied Ned. "I've been trying all morning to like mud and enjoy the smell. Yesterday I even practiced being rude, but it's no good," he sighed. "All the other gnomes laugh at me, you know."

The gnome and the rabbit sat for a while side by side, deep in thought.

"Got it," said the rabbit suddenly. "I think I know where there might be some clean gnomes, although I've only seen them from a distance," she admitted, "so I don't know about the politeness bit."

"Really? Where? Please tell me." The gnome jumped up.

"I'll do better than that, I'll show you. Follow me!" And the rabbit hopped off with Ned following closely behind.

Soon they arrived at the top of a steep hill. Climbing down, they came to a house, the sort that humans live in. Surrounding the house was a garden and in the garden was a large pond. Sitting round the pond were several very clean gnomes.

"Ooh, look at them," said Ned in awe. He left the rabbit nibbling plants and flowers in the garden and went to talk to the gnomes.

"Hello, I'm Ned," he said to a gnome who was sitting holding a tiny fishing rod.

"Sshh," hissed the gnome. "We don't talk during the day, we only talk at night." And with that he sat staring ahead, refusing to say another word.

Going back to the rabbit, Ned explained: "They only talk at night, so I think I'll wait and talk to them then."

"Right-oh," said the rabbit, who had taken quite a liking to Ned. "I'll pop back later and see how you're getting on."

Ned found a large bush near the pond. He wriggled into the centre of it, made himself comfortable and fell asleep.

Later, when the stars were out, Ned woke up. Remembering where he was, he crawled excitedly out of the bush and went up to the gnome he'd spoken to earlier.

"Hello," he said. "My name is Ned."

"Sshh," whispered the gnome, "you'll frighten the fish."

"Can I whisper to you?" whispered Ned.

"If you must," replied the gnome.

In hushed tones Ned explained his problem and said that if they were all nice, clean, polite gnomes, then he would like to join them please. The gnome thought for a while. "O.K.," he said eventually. "My name's Grunt. Go and sit over there," and he pointed to a space between two other gnomes.

29

Ned did as he was told.

"Hello," said Ned to the gnome on his left. "My name is Ned. What's yours?"

"Sshh," said the gnome. "We aren't allowed to talk much in case we disturb the fish, or worse still, wake up the humans."

Ned sat quietly for a while, then, feeling stiff, he got up to stretch his legs.

"Sit still," hissed a voice to his right. "We aren't allowed to move, we might…"

"Disturb the fish," finished Ned. "Yes, I thought as much. Don't you get bored?"

"Of course we don't," whispered the gnome. "We've trained ourselves not to."

Later, the wind started to blow and one of the gnomes fell over, but no one went to help him.

30

"Why doesn't he get up? Is he hurt?" Ned asked the gnome next to him, in surprise.

"No," came the reply. "He's made of plastic, as are some of the others. They belong to the humans."

Ned looked round and thought to himself, "I can't tell the difference."

31

"Do you live like this all the time?" he asked the gnome to his right.

"Of course. It is our job to watch over the fish. We have to protect them."

Ned sat for a while longer. At the far end of the garden he could see that his friend the rabbit had returned. Quietly he left the pond and went over to her.

"I have never been so bored in all my life," he told the rabbit. "My friends might be rude and dirty, and they might smell a bit, but at least they're not boring."

"Time to go home, I think," said the rabbit.

When Ned finally arrived home, everybody made a huge fuss of him. He'd been greatly missed. He told the other gnomes about his adventures and they were all very upset that he had nearly left them and so it was decided that they should make a pact.

It was agreed that no gnome would mind if Ned was clean, sweet smelling and polite, as long as Ned did not mind that the others were sometimes rude, almost always dirty, or that they smelled a bit. After that Ned was never ever tempted to leave his gnome home again, although he did sometimes go for long walks with his special friend the rabbit.

35

GNOME IMPROVEMENTS

WRITTEN BY CLAIRE STEEDEN

In a small garden centre, in a town not far from here, lived a gnome called George. At night, when it was dark and everyone had gone home, George and the rest of his gnome friends played on the swings and slides there and even swam in the pond. They all had lots of fun but were careful that nobody saw them move, hurrying back to their positions before it got light.

One morning, George overheard Sam, the owner, talking to Sarah, who worked there part-time.

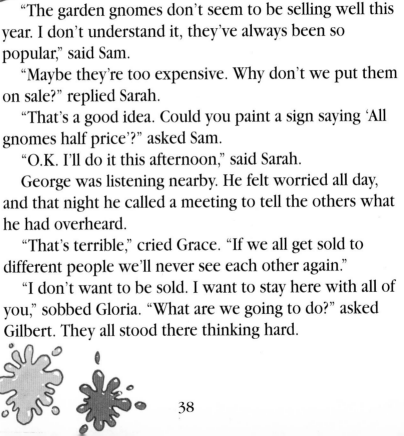

"The garden gnomes don't seem to be selling well this year. I don't understand it, they've always been so popular," said Sam.

"Maybe they're too expensive. Why don't we put them on sale?" replied Sarah.

"That's a good idea. Could you paint a sign saying 'All gnomes half price'?" asked Sam.

"O.K. I'll do it this afternoon," said Sarah.

George was listening nearby. He felt worried all day, and that night he called a meeting to tell the others what he had overheard.

"That's terrible," cried Grace. "If we all get sold to different people we'll never see each other again."

"I don't want to be sold. I want to stay here with all of you," sobbed Gloria. "What are we going to do?" asked Gilbert. They all stood there thinking hard.

38

"We could run away," suggested Gladys.

"But where would we go? We've never been outside the garden centre," said Gerald. "Don't worry," said George. "I think I've got a good idea."

George had watched while Sarah had painted the sale sign. She had used paints and brushes kept in one of the garden sheds.

"Come with me and I'll tell you my plan," said George.

All the gnomes followed George to the shed. "Once we are on sale tomorrow lots of people will want to buy us. They like plain red and white gnomes in their gardens. But if we paint each other in lots of bright colours and patterns we'll look so awful that nobody will want us," explained George.

"That's a brilliant idea," cried Gladys, and all the others agreed. They could hardly wait to get started.

39

They pulled the shed door open and went inside. George climbed up an old wooden ladder and switched the light on.

One by one they opened the tins of paint. Throughout the night they had great fun painting each other in the brightest colours and most outrageous patterns they could think of. George had an orange hat with purple spots, lime green hair, a red and yellow striped jacket, blue trousers with silver stars and the brightest pair of pink boots you have ever seen! The rest of the gnomes looked just as dreadful. As they stood looking at each other, they started to laugh.

"We look awful," cried Grace.

"Nobody will want us in their garden," chuckled Gloria.

"I think we all look marvellous," said Gladys. "Let's just hope nobody else does!"

It was daylight when they finished clearing up — nearly time for Sam and Sarah to arrive for work. They just had time to get to their places and stand still before Sam and Sarah walked through the gate.

Sam took one look at the gnomes and let out a shriek.

"Aarghh, what's happened to the gnomes? We'll never sell them looking like that!"

George winked at the others.

"Some kids must have got in last night and mucked about. But look at the colours they've used! Even at half price nobody will buy them," said Sarah. "Come on, let's have a cup of tea."

All day long the customers remarked on how funny the gnomes looked.

"What a sight. I wouldn't have one in my garden if they were giving them away," said one man.

Then just before closing time an old lady came through the gate.

"Oh my," she cried when she saw the gnomes. "How wonderful! I've got a couple of gnomes in my garden but none as splendid as these."

"You mean you *like* them, madam?" asked Sam.

"Like them? I love them," she replied. "But which one shall I choose?"

On hearing this all the gnomes started to panic. Which one would she buy and take away with her?

"I can't decide," she sighed. "They're all so funny."

"They're half price in our sale, madam," said Sam. "Maybe you'd like more than one."

"What a splendid idea," she said. "In fact, I'll take them all. I can't do much gardening any more so I haven't got many flowers. These gnomes will add a splash of colour and make the garden look more cheerful."

"All of them? Are you sure?" asked Sam.

"Quite sure. It'll be money well spent," replied the lady. Sam took the lady's address so that they could be delivered. Sarah packed them into a big box and put them into the van.

On the way, George whispered to the others, "I don't want to leave the garden centre, but at least we're all together."

When they arrived Sarah carried the box to the front door and rang the bell.

"Oh good. I was hoping you'd be here before dark. I can't wait to put them in the garden," said the old lady.

Sarah carried them through to the back garden. When she had gone the lady carefully unpacked them one by one. When they were all unwrapped she said,

"My name is Daisy. Welcome to my home. It won't be as lonely now with all of you to talk to. It's just a shame you can't talk back."

Daisy put the gnomes around her lovely little garden. When she had finished she stood back to look at them.

"My, you are colourful. You certainly brighten up my garden."

As it was getting dark, Daisy went inside and drew the curtains. After a while the gnomes started to whisper to each other.

"What a pretty garden," said Gilbert

"There's a pond and a swing," said George. "It's probably for her grandchildren."

The other gnomes in the garden introduced themselves, and soon they were all chatting like old friends.

"I think we're going to be very happy living here," said Gladys, smiling.

When Daisy's friends saw the gnomes they wanted some too, so Sarah started to paint the new gnomes at the garden centre. They sold so quickly she could not paint them fast enough. Sam was pleased as business had never been so good, and it was all because of the friendly gnomes who wanted to stay together.

GNOME SWEET GNOME

WRITTEN BY DAN ABNETT

Just west of the snow-capped Candlemass Mountains, at the point where the Great West Road crosses the Green River, you'll find a little pottery business run by a family of gnomes called the Slightlys. These gnomes are kind, generous little people, no taller than a chair leg. They never shout or say rude words or pull hair, they never leave things in a mess and they never have a bad word to say about anyone.

Gnomes are great craftsmen, and the Slightlys are no exception. They have owned the little pottery for years

51

making the finest teapots, bowls, dishes and jugs you'll ever see. Travellers often stop and buy something from the Slightlys' shop. Each item of Gnomeware comes packed in straw in a little wooden box with a label that reads "Slightly Gnome-made".

Mr Slightly is the master potter, and spends all day in the workshop, making the Gnomeware on his potter's wheel. His sister, Everso Slightly, is in charge of the kiln, where she bakes the soft pottery until it's hard. Mrs Slightly and her daughter, Very, paint lovely patterns on the Gnomeware, and glaze them shiny and bright, and Grandma and Grandpa Slightly run the shop.

Then of course, there's young Od. He's Mr Slightly's son, and a fine young figure of a gnome.

It had always been assumed that Od Slightly would follow in the family footsteps and one day become the master potter himself. Everyday, he studied as an apprentice in the workshop. Trouble was, try as he might, Od wasn't very keen on pot-making. He just didn't have his father's patience, or his steady hand. Od's dishes always looked a little wobbly. The handles fell off his jugs, the lids never fitted his bowls, and he was forever getting confused and putting two spouts on his teapots. More than once, he'd lost control of the potter's wheel completely, and sent wet, floppy clay splatting all over the nice clean workshop.

Whenever things went wrong, Od's father would stand with his hands on his hips, shaking his head sadly. Mrs Slightly would say, "There, there, Od," and go and fetch the dustpan and mop. Very Slightly, who could paint patterns on the Gnomeware every bit as well as her mum, would snigger at her brother in a very superior way.

All day long, Od dreamed fantastic dreams of high adventure and peril. He was Od the Pirate Gnome, Od the Jungle Explorer, Od the Racing Car Driver, Od the Test Pilot…He had a stack of old *Ideal Gnome* magazines, which were full of articles about high fliers in the gnome world. Film star gnomes and secret agent gnomes and million pound-transfer footballer gnomes called Gnozza. "One day…" he'd say to himself, as he sponged clay-blobs off the workshop wall, "…one day I'll pack my things, leave this miserable, boring, clay-filled life and go off to seek my fortune. I'll become Very Famous Gnome Celebrity Od Slightly and send exciting postcards home to mum and dad. Just let Very snigger at me then." As an afterthought, he added to himself, "I'll probably have to change my name, though, if I'm going to be a Very Famous Gnome Celebrity. Something like Brad Slightly or Rock Slightly would sound more cool."

55

One particular morning, Od's latest edition of *Ideal Gnome* magazine arrived in the post. In the classified section was an advert that quite took Od's breath away.

"Good-looking young gnomes required for ornamental duties. Apply to the Royal Palace of King Barnabus II."

When Mr Slightly got up for work, he couldn't find Od anywhere. He checked the house and the workshop, but Od was nowhere to be found. Then Aunt Everso found a note pinned to the kiln. "Gone to seek fortune. Have taken clean underwear. Will write soon." It was signed, "Od."

"Oh dear me…" murmured Mrs Slightly.

It took Od three days to reach the palace of King Barnabus II. He was tired and weary by the time he arrived at the gates. If it hadn't been for the lift he'd got for the last ten miles on the back of an ox cart, he was sure he'd never have made it.

The palace was huge, even by gnome standards. Little Od looked around in awe. Big people marched about the place being important. Trumpets blasted out fanfares that made him jump out of his shoes. He had to scurry out of the way of enormous, stomping soldiers, and horses on parade. Even the dwarf footmen looked down on him.

Eventually he found his way to the Lord Chamberlain's office and knocked nervously at the door. "Come in," boomed a deep voice from inside. The chamberlain peered down at him over the top of his glasses with a scornful sneer, and dabbed his pen in the inkpot. "Name?"

"Erm… Shane Slightly," said Od, in a rather shaky voice. He was trembling so hard that his knees knocked together.

"Slightly… hmmm," said the chamberlain, writing it down in a big book. "And you're here for the gnome job?"

"The ornamental one, that's right, sir," said Od with a

friendly grin. The chamberlain didn't smile back. Od didn't really know what the job was about, but he reckoned that if it was ornamental, it probably meant he was going to be a gnome model. Maybe he'd be paid millions and appear on the cover of glamorous fashion magazines. "Follow me," said the chamberlain, and led him through the huge palace gardens and down to the lake. He handed Od a small fishing rod.

"Sit there," he said, pointing to a rock on the lake edge, "and pretend to fish."

"Is that all?" asked Od.

"You'll work from sunrise until sunset, unless there's an evening garden party, in which case you work overtime. On no account are you to move, wander about or do anything except look ornamental." The chamberlain stomped off and left Od to it. Od sat down on the rock, feeling rather uneasy.

Two hours later, he still felt uneasy, but now he felt hot and uncomfortable too. He was bored. His neck was stiff, and there was an annoying fly buzzing around his ear. The Chamberlain came back to check on him.

"Very good, but try smiling too," he said.

"What do I do when I've finished this?" asked Od.

"What do you mean, 'finish'," replied the Chamberlain, looking taken aback. "This is what you're paid to do. You're an ornamental garden gnome."

Od was halfway home, trudging along the Great West Road, when he met Grandpa Slightly coming the other way.

"Thought I might find you out here, young Od," said Grandpa. They fell into step, heading back towards the Candlemass Mountains, where the sun was just setting. "You know, more than anything else, I want to make a big teapot." said Od. "I've really got the urge."

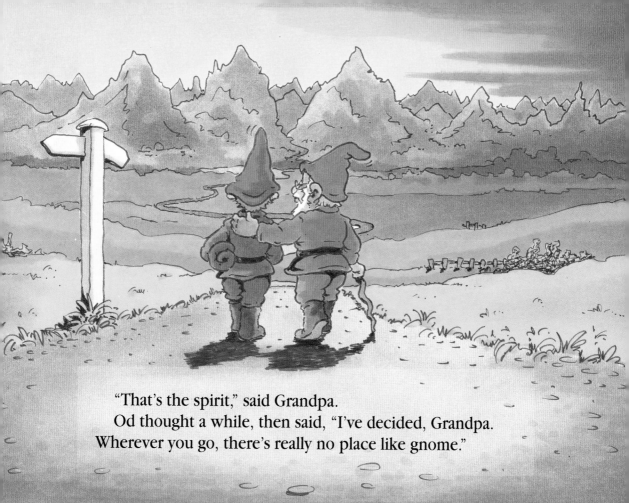

"That's the spirit," said Grandpa.

Od thought a while, then said, "I've decided, Grandpa. Wherever you go, there's really no place like gnome."